This book belongs to

_____

Mia Hamm

By Mary Nhin

Illustrated By
Yuliia Zolotova

Copyright © 2022 by Grow Grit Press LLC. All rights reserved. No part of this book may be reproduced in any form without permission in writing from the publisher. Please send bulk order requests to growgritpress@gmail.com
Paperback ISBN: 978-1-63731-465-4 Hardcover ISBN: 978-1-63731-467-8
Printed and bound in the USA. MiniMovers.tv

Hi, I'm Mia Hamm.

I was born Mariel Margaret Hamm, but people call me Mia. As a kid, I was extremely shy, but sports really helped me express myself.

My older brother, Garrett, helped me nurture my competitive spirit. When we played sports, he always picked me to be on his team even though I was seen as this shy little girl.

Once I found soccer, I played any chance I got! Since we didn't have a soccer field at school, we played on the concrete. This resulted in many skinned knees. I learned how to dribble, trap, and pass on concrete which is a lot harder than playing on grass. I don't remember it being a lot of work, just a lot of fun!

Growing up, I didn't have any soccer female idols to look up to. My teammates and I had to look outside of soccer or to men for sports role models.

Another problem I found was there was not a national women's league for soccer.

Nevertheless, I set goals to achieve.

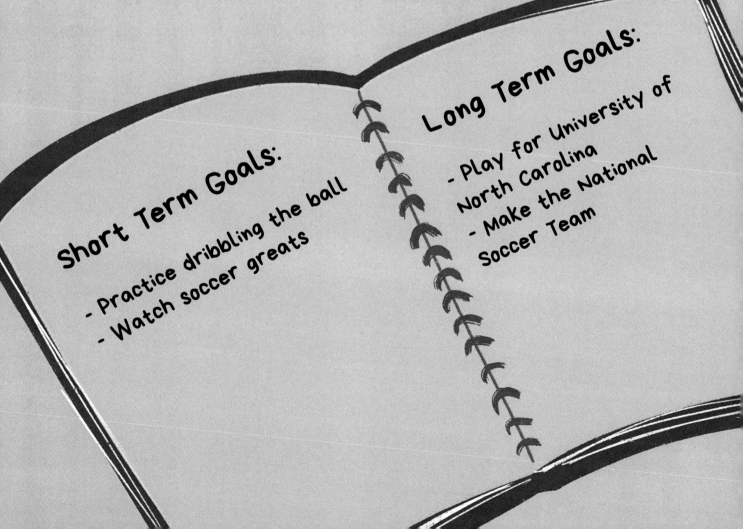

Short Term Goals:
- Practice dribbling the ball
- Watch soccer greats

Long Term Goals:
- Play for University of North Carolina
- Make the National Soccer Team

When I was 15, I joined the women's national soccer team, becoming the youngest person ever to play for the team. I found out quickly I was behind, technically, tactically, and mentally, so I decided to work hard to improve.

I watched great soccer players to increase my understanding of the game, and I put in extra hours dribbling the ball by myself. Sometimes, it was boring, but I loved it.

Remember, this is what sets champions apart. They do what it takes to be the best, no matter how painful, how boring, or how difficult it is to find the time.

For college, I decided to play for North Carolina. During this time, I continued to develop my mental toughness and hard work ethic – getting up early, running sprints, and training with the ball.

One day, my coach left me a note, after seeing me practice by myself.

His words never left my heart, and helped to lift me up and motivate me to work hard when times got tough.

A champion is someone who is bent over, drenched in sweat, at the point of exhaustion when no one else is looking.

While at UNC, I helped our team, the Tar Heels, win four NCAA Division I Women's Soccer Championships in five years.

Then in 1991, our national soccer team made history, by clinching our first World Cup championship title!

In 1996, I played my first Olympic Games in Atlanta. It was the first Olympic tournament to include women's soccer!

Shortly after the Olympics, my brother Garrett passed away and I had a very difficult time. When it was time to compete in my first competition after this tragic event, I had to dig deep to find my mental toughness. Focusing on the present moment and having the support of my teammates helped me to overcome my emotions from the loss of my brother.

In 2000, I became a founding member of the first professional women's soccer league in the United States, the Women's United Soccer Association (WUSA).

I was very excited about what this would mean to young girls everywhere!

You can't control your height or what happens to you, but you can control your effort and attitude. For me, that's what has helped me succeed.

Focus on effort rather than the outcome

Set goals

Work hard

If you can learn to equate effort with success, you will not only be a winner on the field, but through that effort, a winner in life as well.

Timeline

1987 – Mia plays for the United States women's
      national soccer team

1989 – Mia plays for North Carolina and helps team
      win four national championships in five years

1991 – Mia helps team win first World Cup

1996 – Mia competes in Summer Olympic Games

minimovers.tv

 @marynhin   @GrowGrit
#minimoversandshakers

 Mary Nhin   Ninja Life Hacks

 Ninja Life Hacks

 @ninjalifehacks.tv

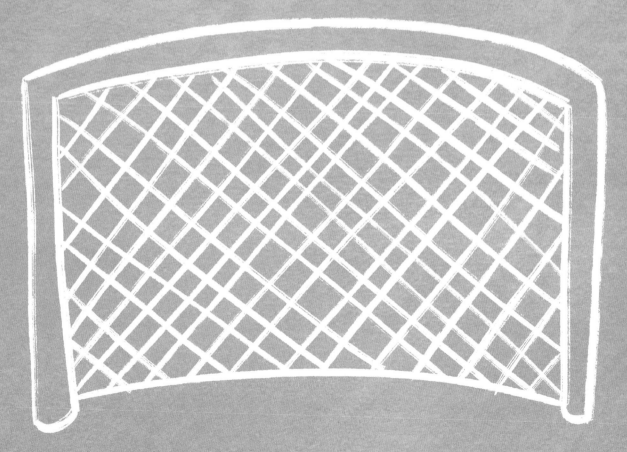

Made in the USA
Las Vegas, NV
08 May 2024

89689040R00024